PRAISE FOR LAUREN CLARK

"Get ready for a great time as you travel along with Julia as she yearns to fall in love with life, family, and syrupy Southern sweet tea."
   - Dina Silver, Author, *One Pink Line*

"Lauren Clark paints a realistic and often hilarious picture of what it's like for a city girl to leave behind her ultra-hectic life and find comfort in a quaint little town in Alabama."
   - Juliette Sobanet, *Kissed in Paris*

"Lauren Clark has definitely been added to my list of favorite authors. "
   - Trudi LoPreto, *Readers Favorite*

"A splash of humor and a healthy dollop of romance make this a fun read from beginning to end."
   - Lynnette Spratley, *Memory's Child*

A VERY DIXIE CHRISTMAS

A NOVELLA

LAUREN CLARK

CAMELLIA PRESS

A VERY DIXIE CHRISTMAS

A NOVELLA

LAUREN CLARK

CAMELLIA PRESS

For Everyone Who Loves a Dixie Christmas

CHAPTER 1

DECEMBER 21

It all started four days before Christmas. And I should have seen it coming.

I'd like to blame Harry Connick, Jr., his dreamy blue eyes, and a voice sweeter than Mama's homemade pecan pie.

I could pin it on the holiday season, the gift-giving excitement, and rounds of glittery, glamorous parties.

I really want to blame my all-out frenzied schedule, lack of sleep, too much coffee, and a work routine that morning blends into night.

But when I look back, it came down to three things. A list, my UPS man, and some mistletoe.

* * *

It's seventy degrees, sunny, with deep cobalt skies that go on forever—an exquisite December day in Eufaula, Alabama. The heavy wooden door to Ella Rae's Sweets, my tiny bakery, is propped wide open in welcome.

As the melodies from "Sleigh Ride" and "Let it Snow" drift out to the street, I find it impossible not to hum along.

Though I know the words to every song, I bite my bottom lip and giggle instead.

Though I love to sing, once I hit a few enthusiastic, off-key notes, my customers might decide to shop elsewhere, so I let Harry Connick, Jr. take center stage. There's something infectious about a Southern boy and New Orleans charm that makes everyone's heart happy.

It's been a wonderfully busy few hours, and it's my first moment to breathe after this morning's rush of customers. I pause to enjoy the peace, drinking in a few moments of solace with my first sip of coffee since seven o'clock.

I glance around the shop, trying not to pinch myself that I really own this bright and adorable establishment. The stainless steel appliances gleam, the countertops shine, and my bakery case is full of treats. Knowing it's been a lifelong dream to own my own business, my brother, Shug, and my grandmother helped finance the venture last year. We celebrated our one year anniversary in April.

You can find the shop downtown, tucked to the side of the historic brick Reeves Peanut Company building on East Broad Street. It's less than four miles from my house on Magnolia, and I grin every time I turn off Randolph Street and see the cheery yellow and blue sign. The lettering is swirly and perfect, finished off with the outline of a cupcake topped with a twist of frosting.

Inside, the shop holds six cafe tables and matching chairs. This year, I've gone all out for the holiday season, draping white lights along the pressed-tin ceiling, hanging an old wooden sled and reindeer decorations on the walls. I've grouped pink and red poinsettias in every corner, and paper whites grace every table.

My daughter, Ella Rae, helped me choose and decorate the tree in the front picture window. We hung silver cookie cutters from the branches, strung green and red candied popcorn, and topped off the petite Scotch Pine with a star fashioned out of pipe cleaners and glued-on peppermint hard candies.

The store is named for my precious (and very precocious) eight-year old, who's sitting at the table closest to the counter. One hand grips her pink Hello Kitty pencil, the other's lost in a halo of dark ringlets. She's hard at work on her Christmas list, a task which she's promised to finish by suppertime.

"Mama, how do you spell 'accessories?'" asks Ella Rae.

I pause from kneading pie dough, allowing a dusting of flour to rest on my fingertips. *Accessories? What in the world is she putting on Santa's list?*

Keeping a straight face, I don't ask, though I'm dying to know. "A-c-c-e-s-s-o-r-i-e-s," I say.

My daughter nods, copying letter for letter with the utmost care. "Thank you." Ella Rae flashes a dimpled smile and bends her head back down, concentrating on the paper laid out on the circular table.

"Almost done?" I ask, taking up the rolling pin to press the dough evenly.

She pauses to take a sip of her hot chocolate. The drink's piled high with swirls of homemade whipped cream—just the way she likes it—and my daughter comes away with a frothy white mustache. "A few more to go." she says.

"Okay." I wink at Ella Rae, hiding a shiver of worry, and steal a glance at the clock.

A hand-written Santa list has been a Jordan family tradition since I was a little girl, and this can't be the year we miss out. Like I did as a child, in the weeks leading up to Christmas, my daughter writes down her most-wanted gifts—keeping them all a secret. When she's finished, she folds up the list, slips it in an envelope, and addresses it to the North Pole. We walk the sealed letter to the post office, hand in hand, and when she's ready, Ella Rae kisses the back for luck, and slips it inside the mailbox.

We usually have plenty of time for her letter to get from Eufaula, Alabama to Santa and his elves, even with a blizzard, Nor'easter, or freak storm. This year, though there's no natural disaster, we're bumping up against Father Time.

The list should have been done weeks ago. Now, I have ninety-six hours, and not a clue about what's at the top of Ella Rae's paper. I frown and think about the small pile of toys hidden in the back of my bedroom closet. One My Little Pony—Princess Alicorn Twilight Sparkle, a pink softball mitt for the spring, a hardcover set of *Little House on the Prairie* books, and a Barbie convertible.

Those are the easy gifts, the ones she's mentioned a few times throughout the year, items she's lingered over in the Dothan Barnes & Noble and local toy stores.

But Ella Rae—being my child, and taking after me in a creative, stubborn way—always comes up with a humdinger. The year's most coveted gift is typically something a mom can't find in any department store, order online, or pick up at a gift shop.

Two years ago, it was sparkly red shoes and a blue and white checked dress exactly like Dorothy's from *The Wizard of Oz*, special-ordered from an Atlanta children's boutique. No knock-off shoes or costumes bought from Party City; my daughter would know the difference.

Last year, she asked for a pony. Thank goodness a borrowed, chocolate brown quarter horse ended up being even better than the real thing. After new cowgirl boots, a dozen lessons at Hillside Ranch, and a few dust-filled days watching barrel racing and roping, Ella Rae decided she didn't want to be a rodeo stunt rider, after all.

I consider myself lucky she hasn't asked for a baby brother or sister. Knowing Ella Rae, she would demand to know why a wiggling bundle of joy wasn't under the tree, then insist on being taken to the North Pole to file a complaint with the elves, Mrs. Claus, and the man in red himself.

Smiling at the thought and shaking my head, I turn back to my own list—a staggering run-down of holiday treats to finish and package before the big brown UPS truck and my trusty delivery man, Daniel, arrive this afternoon.

I rub my neck, trying to ease the tension, and remind myself that tomorrow's list isn't quite as daunting. Three chess pies for Miss Pam Snead at Shorter Mansion, a red velvet cake for Miss Janie White, and two dozen Pillow Pocket Puffs for Mr. Doug Winkleblack's holiday party.

For any last minute shoppers, my bakery shelves are stocked with creamy Pralines, Hummingbird Cake, sugar and spice cookies, and banana pudding. For the holidays, I've added Sweet Potato Buttermilk Pie, Eggnog Pound Cake, Gingerbread Soufflés, reindeer cookies, and Santa cake pops in a variety of colors and flavors.

The first few notes of "Sleigh Ride" begin to play, and I hum along as I start my next task. Laying my buttery pie dough in a row of tins, I trim and crimp the edges as I move from one to the next. My chocolate pecan tarts have become a local favorite, and I spoon the dark confection carefully into each waiting dish.

The smell of caramelized sugar, toasted nuts, and a hint of vanilla waft up and tickle my nose. It's one of my favorite parts of baking, the individual flavors and textures melding together to form something sweet and savory.

I also love the thought that my pies and cakes are, somehow, a small part of local families' celebrations. It's my hope, that in the future, Ella Rae's Sweets will be known for delicious desserts that can be enjoyed every holiday or special occasion for generations to come.

As I pop the finished tarts in the oven to bake and crank my timer to buzz in exactly one hour, I lean over the counter, and reach for my pen. With a surge of satisfaction, I cross one more order off my very long list.

My iPod soundtrack shifts to another of my all-time favorite Christmas tunes, Bruce Springsteen's rendition of 'Santa Claus is Comin' to Town.'

My eyes meet Ella Rae's and we grin. She jumps up from the table, and this time, I crank up the volume. The shop's empty, so I grab my daughter's hand and pull her to the center of the room. Using my wooden spoon for a mic, I lip sync along with The Boss, then step back when it's Ella Rae's turn to do air-saxophone, mimicking Clarence with perfect timing.

Breathless, we giggle at the end of the song and I clap for my daughter, who takes a bow, sweeping her arm grandly below her waist.

"So, darlin'," I say casually. "Santa Claus *is* Comin' to Town...in a couple of days. Got that list done?"

Flopping back down into her cafe chair, Ella Rae rubs her nose and knits her brow. "Oh, I can't decide, Mama."

My joyful holiday spirit evaporates just a bit. I tamp down the panic rising in my chest. The slight neurosis about Christmas is hereditary.

During my childhood, my own mother, Aubie, spent months preparing for Christmas morning. Stockings hung, cookies baked, presents wrapped. Everything perfect and ahead of schedule. Enough perfection to make any daughter paranoid. Throw in the possibility of breaking family tradition, and I might not live until New Year's Eve.

I get a slight reprieve from my anxiety when the bell over the front door jingles. I glance up and wave at Linda and Ted Hicks. They're a wonderful couple, married for many years, with a loving family full of children and grandchildren.

Ted's an architect with Blondheim & Mixon downtown on East Broad Street. He has a great personality; always quick to smile and share a joke. His wife, Linda, gorgeous in a classic way, is an elegant Southern woman who's as kind as she is generous.

"Hey, y'all," I call out. I crane my neck, looking for Arthur Cunningham, the eight-year-old boy who usually tags along with the Hicks on most Saturday afternoons.

"Happy-almost Christmas," Ted says, grinning. He pauses to ruffle Ella Rae's hair. She jumps up and gives him a squeeze, looking like a pixie next to his towering frame. Ted lowers her back into her seat and eyes my daughter's list.

Ella Rae giggles and covers it up with both hands.

Ted winks at me. "She on the nice or naughty list?

It takes Linda half a second to jab her husband in the ribs. "Theodore Hicks," she whispers, looking mortified and amused at the same time. "You apologize this instant."

"Mr. Ted, I'm on the 'nice' list, sir," Ella Rae pipes up, puffing out her small chest. "I've been really, really good this year. Ask Mama."

Three pairs of eyes land on me. All I can do is break into a huge grin and shrug. "She has been. Santa should be proud."

Linda smiles at Ella Rae. "That's great, PD."

For all of you SEC fans, PD's my nickname. Mama and Daddy graduated from Auburn University, known throughout the Deep South as a sports powerhouse. In honor of the school's football program, they named me after coach Pat Dye. My brother, likewise, carries on the legacy of coach Shug Jordan. We're no relation to either man, just proud to be associated with such championship-level leaders.

Though Ted and Linda root for rival University of Alabama, we can agree on our love for Eufaula, delicious Christmas sweets, and steaming hot coffee.

"Can I get you the usual?" I ask, starting to reach for two mugs.

They nod, and Ted puts his arm around Linda. "And I'd like the 10% discount," he says, leaning over to plant a kiss on his wife's lips.

"You've got it," I chirp, blushing pink at their sweet display of affection.

A few weeks ago, as a joke, Shug hung a sprig of mistletoe above the counter and made a huge sign offering 10% off any order when accompanied by a kiss.

No one was more surprised when my customers didn't laugh—they all fell in love with the idea. In a day, word spread all over town, and the *Eufaula Tribune* sent a reporter over to the bakery to cover the story. An article featuring my brother's brilliant idea appeared on the front page of last Sunday's paper.

Staying safely behind the counter, I've yet to be kissed, but it's sure been fun watching even the stodgiest of couples melt a little when they smooch under the bakery's mistletoe.

If I had to add it all up, I'd say Shug's idea has netted the bakery at least an extra three hundred dollars in profits and paid out five times that much in happiness.

Arm-in-arm, Ted and Linda take the window seat looking out on East Broad Street. Outside, Christmas lights twinkle red and green in the fading sunlight.

Quickly, I mix up Linda's non-fat white chocolate latte and pour Ted's dark roast into a tall ceramic mug. He drinks it black and loves Jamaican Blue Mountain, which happens to be today's featured flavor.

"Enjoy," I say and set their drinks on the counter. "And would you try some of my new Rum Raisin cake? You can be my first taste-testers!" I select two plump slices from a long ceramic dish on the counter and place them carefully on doily-covered plates.

"Now, PD, we shouldn't—" Linda begins, then laughs as Ted shushes her.

Balancing everything on a tray, I walk over to deliver the steaming drinks and dessert. Ted takes the first plate from me and sets it in front of his wife. As I carefully set the silverware and napkins on the table, Linda smiles up at Ted and squeezes his hand as they settle in to enjoy their dessert and coffee.

"Hope you like it," I whisper, and tiptoe back to the counter.

They're so adorable.

It's clear that their love is forever, like a storybook romance come to life. Their marriage—Ted's devotion, Linda's contentment—gives me hope. Knights in shining armor do exist. Real men will slay dragons for the women they love. And there can be a happily ever after.

With a slight sigh, I consider my own relationships. I've definitely kissed more than a few frogs, including Ella Rae's father.

s I've told all of my friends, I'm still waiting for my prince.

Until then, I have my boyfriend of the moment, Billy Bob Mullins.

Billy, whose adoration for deer and dove hunts rivals all other basic instincts, including oxygen, food, and sleep.

The bell over the door jingles a second time, forcing my mind back to the present.

A small, crimson-clad shape rushes by the counter. This time, it is Arthur Cunningham, breathing hard. He presses a hand to his heart as if to protect the muscle from jumping through his skin.

"Thought I'd missed y'all," Arthur says, bending to cough. Ella Rae's classmate and known school trouble-maker, lives down the street from the Hicks family on Magnolia Street.

Like me, Arthur's mama is single. His daddy took off about the same time Ella Rae's father disappeared. We're not close friends, but she's a hard worker, and a kind person, struggling to make ends meet.

From what Linda's mentioned—which isn't a lot—

Arthur's mother isn't home much. She works two jobs to put food on the table. During the day, she waits tables at the Honeysuckle Cafe. At night, she has a housekeeping position at the Best Western hotel. Both minimum wage, both draining. I'm not sure when the woman sleeps, except on days like today.

While his mother steals an afternoon nap on Saturdays, Arthur tags along with the Hicks. Though Linda and Ted would gladly buy him anything his heart desired in the entire shop, he never asks for more than one dessert, and takes his time to decide.

I can usually count on fifteen minutes for Arthur to peruse the shelves of pastries, occasionally asking questions about each selection and tasting a sample.

On purpose, I save a few 'damaged' bars and 'broken' cookies every week, citing that they can't possibly be sold. They end up in a plain white bag, sometimes filled, sometimes half-filled, and go home with Arthur to share with his mother.

The oven buzzer sounds and I hurry to retrieve the goodies.

"Be right back, Arthur," I call over my shoulder. He's standing square in front of the baking rack, examining today's offerings with great reverence.

Today, among a dozen other recipes, I'm trying my second batch of salted toffee pecan bars. When I open the door, the scent of nuts and brown sugar fills the shop. After donning heavy black oven mitts, I place the trays on cooling racks.

Tara and Robert Bennett came in earlier and bought an entire pan for an office celebration. This afternoon, I'm shipping another dozen to my sweet friend Lora Campbell Roberts in Odenville, Alabama, just outside Birmingham.

I'd saved samples for Arthur and Ella Rae to try. I offer

the plate of morsels over the baking rack. "Here, Arthur, try these, honey."

In typical Arthur fashion, he crinkles his nose, shakes his hair off his face and considers this.

After another half second, he snatches up a toffee bar.

He pops a few pieces in his mouth, chews thoughtfully and closes his eyes, savoring the flavors. When his dark doe-brown eyes pop open, he peppers me with questions.

"What makes these so chewy?" and "Why use pecans and not walnuts?" followed by "Do you have to put salt in them and how much?"

I smother a laugh. It's typical Arthur Cunningham.

"They're chewy because of the amount of butter, sugar, and flour that I mix together," I say. "I use pecans because they're very traditional and Southern, so I like them best." I take a breath. "And the salt balances out the sweetness. It's kind of like eating buttered popcorn and then having M&Ms every couple of bites—but doing it all at once."

I catch Ella Rae's eye. "Want some, sweetie?"

But she doesn't answer me. Her brow is knit together.

"Arthur, why do you ask so many questions?" Ella Rae asks. She puts down her pen and studies her classmate.

Arthur ponders this for a moment and wanders over to her corner of the room.

I fight the urge to quiet my daughter but am semi-fascinated by their adolescent banter. I notice that's Ted's amused, but quickly goes back to his Jamaican roast. Linda sips her latte and, like me, keeps listening.

"I like facts," Arthur says. "I want to know the truth about things. I like to know why."

"Why?" Ella Rae asks again.

"Because," Arthur shoots back.

Ella Rae shrugs and goes back to working on her list. I breathe a sigh of relief. Arthur has a reputation for being a bit overbearing. He's bright. Smarter than anyone gives him credit for—mostly because the clothes he wears are often a size too small and his shoes are worn with holes.

He quotes statistics from *Popular Science* and *Myth Busters* and memorizes facts and figures with amazing speed. I distinctly remember that by age four, Arthur could recite all of the American presidents up to Abraham Lincoln, including their middle names.

Lately, Arthur's been hooked on everything related to geometry and physics. If he stays on track and in school, despite the economic odds against him, I fully expect him to graduate from MIT at the age of sixteen.

In comparison, Ella Rae's the dreamer. She makes up stories, creates dragons out of clouds, and is forever looking for secret hiding places and trap doors in our little bungalow. She lives for books like *The Spiderwick Chronicles*. Full of imagination and possibilities.

Though the day is coming, I'm not about to thrust the sting of adulthood on my child and snuff out her imagination.

That is, until Arthur Cunningham messes with that plan, threatens to derail my deadline, and destroy my family tradition. Maybe forever.

It's like watching an automobile crash in slow motion, and not being able to do a thing to prevent it.

"What are you doing?" he asks, straining to see Ella Rae's project.

My daughter straightens up and cocks her head to one side, deciding whether or not to answer. "Finishing a letter," she says, moving her elbow to cover up the words. The movement sweeps her carefully lettered envelope to the ground. It flutters and lands at Arthur's feet.

He frowns, reads the address, and then his eyes widen.

"You're writing a Christmas list to Santa?" he asks. His voice contains the disdain of a jaded adult.

I clamp my lips shut, trying to decide whether or not to interrupt. Ted and Linda have already turned their heads.

"Yes," says Ella Rae. She meets Arthur's gaze. "Please give it back." She holds out her palm for the envelope.

Arthur sweeps his hand to the floor, scoops it up, and hands it back over. "Santa Claus isn't real." He jabs his fists into his sides.

There's a gasp of dismay from across the room and Linda half-rises from her chair. Ted murmurs something and pats his wife's hand. Slowly, she sinks back into her seat.

I'm frozen to the counter, torn between defending the magic of the holiday season with allowing my daughter to fight her own battles. Pressing my fingernails into my palm, I go through the motions of making another batch of pie dough.

Ella Rae's staring at her classmate, eyes narrowed.

"Think about it," Arthur continues. "If Santa Claus exists, he has to deliver presents to two-hundred-million kids all over the world."

"There are more kids than that," Ella Rae retorts. "There's like...two billion. We learned that at school."

I flush with pride at my daughter standing up for herself.

"Not everyone celebrates Christmas," Arthur says, folding his arms across his chest. "Some people have Hanukah or Kwanza. Or they don't believe in it at all."

Ella Rae and I both deflate. He's right.

"But, there's a guy at North Carolina State who says it's possible for Santa Claus to do it." Arthur stops to roll his eyes. "So, according to him, if Santa's sleigh stopped at seventy-five million homes in twenty-four hours, the sleigh'd have to go five million miles an hour."

Ella Rae shrinks down a bit more. I resist running across

the room and throwing my arms around her. She can stand up to him, I tell myself, and cling to the counter instead.

Arthur taps his fingers on one arm. "But, then, this professor and his students decided that traveling that fast is impossible. So, now they say that Santa uses relativity clouds."

"Clouds?" Ella Rae echoes, scrunching up her nose in doubt.

"Yeah, the clouds *supposedly* stretch time like a rubber band," says Arthur, raising an eyebrow. "That'd give Santa months to deliver gifts. To us, it'd just seem like a few minutes went by."

My daughter's eyes fill with tears. "He has helpers. He has elves. Lots of them. And maybe more sleighs and reindeer."

At the sight of Ella Rae so upset, Ted Hicks jumps up. "And all of those helper sleighs probably have jet packs." He squeezes her shoulder. "And folks here on the ground to pick up the slack." Arthur shakes his head.

I can't hold back another second. I dash over to my daughter and sink down to my knees. "I believe he's real, Ella Rae. All sorts of things are possible. Sometimes you can't explain everything. Especially the magic at Christmastime."

"It's not true," Arthur interrupts. "Magic isn't real either."

"That's enough," Ted says gently, steering Arthur toward the door.

I'm in shock. I've never seen Arthur act like this. He's smart. Wise beyond his years. But to ruin Christmas for everyone else isn't fair.

Ella Rae stands up. "You're wrong, Arthur."

"I'm not. And I'll prove it," he says, shaking loose of Ted's grasp. "Every year I've asked Santa Claus for a Lego set."

My daughter wrinkles her forehead. "A Lego set?"

"Not just any Lego set," Arthur snorts. "The Harry Potter Hogwarts Castle with twelve-hundred and ninety pieces.

The one with Voldemort, Dumbledore, and Snape. It even has the Sorting Hat, Gryffindor's Sword, and secret sliding stairs," Arthur adds wistfully. "For the last four years, I've sent a letter to the North Pole."

My daughter is silent.

Arthur folds his arms across his chest. "Then, Christmas morning. Nothing."

CHAPTER 3

DECEMBER 21

*I*t's been an hour since Ted, Linda, and Arthur Cunningham left the shop, and Ella Rae still refuses to discuss it.

"Sweetheart?" I plead with her for the fifth time. "Let's talk."

Finally, Ella Rae shakes her head, snatches up her list, and stomps out of the room.

There's nothing I can do to reach her right now. She grabs her iPod, crams in her ear buds, and curls up in my office on her pink bean bag chair. When she realizes that I'm still standing in the doorway, she pulls her purple fleece blanket up to her chin and closes her eyes.

I walk away slowly, rubbing my temples, and head for the kitchen, waiting for divine intervention or some force of parental wisdom to hit me.

None comes.

Then, the oven buzzer sounds, loud and shrill.

I jump at the noise and sniff the air. A thin trail of smoke leaks from the oven.

The tarts are burning.

I snatch open the oven door, cram a thick, black mitt on my hand and yank at the tray. I jerk too hard and send the tarts flying across the room.

Like projectiles, the circular tins fly out in an arc and land around my feet, crusts breaking into crumbled pieces. All of my hard work. Wasted.

Near tears, I shake off the oven mitt, bend my knees, and begin picking up crumbs with my bare fingers. Melted chocolate sears my fingers.

"Youch!" I yelp. My skin burns and I drop the mess back on the tile. Closing my eyes, I sit on the floor, cross my ankles, and tuck my legs close to my body. Rocking back and forth, I begin to cry. Exactly when Daniel's UPS truck rumbles up outside the bakery.

Just like always, he honks the horn once, retrieves any deliveries from inside the van, and bounds inside the shop. I even know the sound of his work boots as he strides across the bakery floor. If I had to guess, he's wearing a smile wide enough to break open Jack Frost's frozen heart.

"PD?" he calls out.

I choke back a sob and don't answer, burying my face between my knees. I should answer. I can tell from the sound of his voice that he's worried.

Daniel's a sweetheart, literally the boy next door growing up on Magnolia Street. His family moved to town the first day of second grade in Moorer Middle School.

On the day we met, I was in the front row with a huge, ridiculous pink bow in my hair. He sat in the back with a crew cut and plaid shirt. At recess, when the school bully made fun of the mass of curled ribbon on my head, Daniel clocked him in the jaw. I swooned. He took detention like a champ. We've been best friends ever since.

Finally, Daniel's boots clunk across the floor. He leans over and switches off the oven timer. *Thank you Jesus.*

"I'm down here," I say in an almost-whisper.

The moment he turns and looks, the fire alarm begins to wail.

Daniel goes into emergency mode. In a flash, he's beside me on the floor, taking my hand in his. "PD, come on. You have to get up."

I try to focus on his blue eyes, but the piercing shriek of the siren makes my brain hurt.

"Mama!" Ella Rae runs into the kitchen, eyes wide. "Is there a fire?"

"Everything's fine, sweetie," I say, taking her hand while Daniel guides us out the front door. "I've got this," he says.

Ella Rae and I sink onto the bench outside. I reach an arm around her shoulders and tuck her in close. Over my shoulder, I can see Daniel waving smoke away from the alarm with a round silver tray. He's opened the back door, letting the ceiling full of gray clouds float up, outside, and away.

Five minutes later, he waves us back into the store. "I think it's finally safe," he says, grinning.

"Thank you," I say, standing up. I'm so grateful, and suddenly exhausted. Ella Rae doesn't say a word, just walks back inside with her head down.

I must look mournful because Daniel doesn't say another word, just wraps me in his arms. He holds me against his chest, and for a moment, I let myself lean against the warmth of his body, inhaling the scent of his skin, now laced with smoke, dark chocolate, and pastry dough.

"What happened?" he murmurs into my hair. His hand slides down my back, pulling me closer.

Suddenly, I realize that I'm standing on the sidewalk for God and country to see, wrapped in an embrace with my UPS man. I wriggle free, gasping for air, wondering if all of my good sense burned into the atmosphere along with my pecan tarts.

"It-it's fine. I-I was in a hurry, didn't pay attention, and set the timer for too long," I stutter, smoothing my apron and looking away at the sky, the cement, and the brick of my building. "It's nothing I can't redo."

My face burns. When I finally lift my chin and meet his eyes, Daniel is staring at me strangely. He knows there's more to the story.

"PD—" he says.

I press my lips together and refuse to explain.

"Come on back inside," he murmurs, edging toward the door. "Don't you have a few packages for me?"

My hand flies to my mouth. "Oh, no. I've made you late." I wince when we step back inside and I see the time. Daniel's usually out until almost midnight on his rural route. Christmas is his busiest time of year.

I rush to wrap my deliveries, adding tissue paper for cushioning, attaching the pre-filled labels, and taping the boxes closed. "Where's...?" I can't think of his helper's name.

Daniel sees me glance at the truck. "Rodney?" he prompts me. "Called in sick. I don't expect he'll be in Monday or Tuesday night either." He slaps his chest with one hand. "Just me this Christmas. But never fear. I'll get 'er done."

His out-of-character Southern slang makes me giggle.

"Okay." I slide the stack across the counter. "Thank you," I say, meaning for everything. Cleaning the mess, airing out my bakery. For making me smile.

"Always," Daniel replies. He glances around the room, looking for my daughter. "Bye, Ella Rae," he calls out.

No reply.

"I'm sorry. She's upset," I say. "Arthur Cunningham told her there isn't a Santa Claus," I confess.

Daniel nods, now understanding why I burned the tarts. "Why'd he go and do that?"

"No Lego Hogwarts Castle under his tree," I say, raising an eyebrow. "For the past few years." I lower my voice and raise up on my tiptoes, looking to see if Ella Rae's hiding around the corner, eavesdropping. "He made a list. Sent it to the North Pole. And nothing." I whisper the rest. "So he made fun of Ella Rae for her letter to Santa."

"I see," says Daniel. He sticks a hand in his pocket and withdraws a piece of paper. Carefully, he unfolds it, enough so that I recognize the loopy writing. "A letter. Like this one?"

It's Ella Rae's.

"That's mine!" A voice behind me announces.

I shriek and clap both hands to my chest. "Ella Rae Sweet," I yell. "You scared me half to death." I gasp, trying to slow my racing heart.

"Mr. Daniel, may I have it?" Ella Rae ignores me and marches in between us, palm outstretched.

He nods solemnly and hands the list to my daughter.

"Thank you." Taking two steps away, she turns her back to us, and rips the list to shreds, letting the pieces flutter to the floor like snowflakes.

"Ella Rae," I scold.

Daniel puts a finger to his lips and motions for me to let her finish.

When the final scrap falls at her feet, Daniel bends down beside my daughter. "Your mama told me what Arthur said."

Ever so slightly, Ella Rae nods.

"That must have hurt your feelings," he adds.

My heart twists with pain when she doesn't reply.

"You know, Christmas magic only happens when you really believe in it. When you wish and pray for good things to come—not just to you, but to your family and neighbors," says Daniel. "Sometimes, you even have to wish for a little happiness for people who aren't very nice to us." "But why?" Ella Rae's voice is small and dark.

Daniel pats my daughter's hand. "Because that's the only way joy spreads. One person has to pass it to another. And that person passes it to another person. It's why Christmas is called the season of *giving*."

Ella Rae nods.

"And it doesn't have to be a present, especially for us big people," Daniel continues. "Sometimes, you can give someone a smile, say kind words, or give a hug. My mama's favorite thing was to get a card on Christmas morning. One from me, one from my sister. We'd always write her a special note and draw her pictures."

"That's all she wanted?" Ella Rae asks.

"It's what made her happy," he replies. "Santa Claus takes care of the rest for children. Even without a list." He taps his temple with his index finger. "Santa already knows."

Ella Rae glances back at me with a thoughtful expression, then turns to Daniel. "But, do toys get lost sometimes?"

Daniel scratches his chin. "Sometimes, my packages do get lost. It doesn't happen very often, and we don't *want* it to happen, but a few times, deliveries get sent to the wrong person." He gazes at my daughter steadily. "It might take a while, but we always try to fix it. Get the package to the right person, even if it takes a month or a year."

"A whole year?" Ella Rae repeats, her mood brightening immensely. I can almost see the wheels turning inside her brain. Thinking about Arthur, Lego Hogwarts Castles, and UPS delivery trucks.

"Yep." Daniel stands up and brushes off his pants. He tugs at one of Ella Rae's curls. "Now, isn't it time for you girls to get home?"

Whistling, Daniel sweeps my packages off the counter, and waves goodbye. "See y'all Monday." And he's gone.

As his truck rolls out of sight, I turn off the shop lights, and help my daughter wriggle into her jacket.

Then, in the quiet, one anxious, terrifying thought hits me square between the eyes.

I never asked Daniel what was written on the top of Ella Rae's list to Santa.

After tossing and turning all night, I wake up with the sunrise and begin baking again. I have a few hours before church, and plan on making pie crust so that it's ready to go for this afternoon.

As I pull out the butter, flour, salt, and sugar, lining them up on my counter, my thoughts immediately fly to last night. To Arthur Cunningham, Ella Rae, Ted and Linda Hicks. And, of course, Daniel.

Surely, Daniel noticed what was written at the top of Ella Rae's list. A word, a phrase, anything that'll give me a clue.

I slide my eyes to the clock on the wall. It's way to early to call. The man is a UPS driver. He's by himself on his route. It's the busiest time of the year. And Sunday is his one day off.

Shaking my head, as if to tell myself no, I bend to get out my mixing bowls, measuring cups, and spoons.

My heart starts racing.

If Daniel knows what Ella Rae wants, I could send Aubie to get it this afternoon—on the off chance it's not a Koala Bear from Australia—which would be my luck.

She would even have time to drive to Dothan, or Columbus, Georgia. Atlanta, if I promised to make it up to her. It would probably mean dressing Billy in a jacket and tie and dragging him to Sunday dinner, where he'd sit though three hours of grueling questions, courtesy of my mother. He'd be stuffed full of fried chicken, collard greens, and sweet tea, but the man might never speak to me again in this lifetime.

I pick up a stick of butter and begin to unwrap it.

I could text Daniel.

He might not be asleep.

And if he is, he won't be that angry.

I stop unwrapping, set the butter down, wipe off my hands, and grab my iPhone. I scroll through my list of names, find Daniel, and start typing.

"Urgent! Need to know if you saw # 1 on list."

I wait a minute. No answer.

"Ella's list? Please help."

Nothing.

"Are you asleep? Did you see Ella's list?"

I pace the kitchen, swinging my arms back and forth, waiting for my phone to vibrate.

Two more minutes go by.

And then another.

I check my phone to make sure that it hasn't suddenly died on me.

As soon as I touch the screen, my own messages stare back at me.

I send one more for good measure. "9-1-1. Ella Rae. List. Am panicking."

That should do it.

I press the phone to my heart and close my eyes. Five seconds later, my iPhone buzzes. I nearly jump out of my skin in relief.

Blinking, I scan the message from Daniel.

"Emergency at work." There's a long pause.

"No worries about gift."

No worries? Does that mean he knows? Or that he's going to dream up a spectacular present?

I'm about to text back when a third message comes through.

"Have a plan."

Eyebrows raised, I try to interpret the words.

He has a plan? I have a plan? We need a plan.

Absolutely nothing comes to mind—other than shaking some sense into that little Arthur Cunningham—but even scaring the tar out of him with the Abominable Snowman won't help a bit at this point.

With a sigh, I put the phone down on the tabletop and rub my temples with my fingers.

I take a breath.

I have work to do. And I have to trust Daniel. He's never let me down before.

As I measure and combine the flour, salt, and sugar in my food processor, I think about how my best friend so easily handled last night's conversation with Ella Rae.

He knows how much Christmas means to me. How much I'd like Ella Rae to keep believing in the joy and magic of the holiday season.

I'm used to the stress of being a single mom, but the pressure of growing my business and making sure everyone else's holiday season is merry and bright has been a challenge to manage—without the worry of someone ruining Ella Rae's Christmas.

Using a new package of chilled butter from the refrigerator, I chop the sticks into small pieces and add it to the mixture. I pulse a half dozen more times until the ingredients resemble coarse meal. Next, I add ice water, one tablespoon at a time, mixing until the dough just begins to hold together.

I check with my fingers, pressing and molding.

Perfect. It's ready.

I click off the Kitchen Aid, pull out the dough, and gently shape the dough mixture into two disks. Dusting them lightly with flour, I secure each tightly in plastic wrap and place them in the refrigerator.

Closing the door behind me, I turn and press my back to the cold surface.

I force myself to exhale.

Everything's going to be fine.

Except that my daughter, sooner or later, will want proof. A small miracle. A wow factor, preferably in the form of something tangible.

And now I only have three days.

CHAPTER 5

*A*fter Ella Rae wakes up, showers and dresses in her Sunday best, it's off to church for both of us. As we sit down in our regular pew, fourth row from the front on the right side of First Baptist Church of Eufaula, I pray for forgiveness right away.

Dear Lord, please understand that my mind is on the coming of Baby Jesus today, but I am a tiny bit distracted by the thought of Ella Rae being disappointed this holiday season.

Please give me patience and help me not burn anymore pecan tarts. I need special help, Holy Father, keeping track of all of my orders and getting them delivered on time.

Lastly, forgive me for wanting to strangle Arthur Cunningham for hurting Ella Rae's feelings. Help me to spread joy and love into his heart...somehow. And please, above everything else, Lord God, let me come up with a miracle to make Ella Rae's Christmas her happiest ever.

The congregation stands then, and I catch Daniel's eye. He's across the aisle with his sister, focused on the preacher. I force my eyes on the hymnal and sing along but find that I can't concentrate on anything but the edge of Daniel's dark blue suit.

I follow the edge of the material along his broad shoulders, letting my gaze fall on the white collar of his shirt and the bright red of his tie. How have I never before noticed that Daniel—my best friend and UPS man—is handsome? Really handsome.

Then, as if he knows I'm looking, he flashes me a brilliant smile.

"We have to talk," I mouth urgently, standing on my tiptoes and trying not to gesture across the aisle.

"Mama," Ella Rae tugs on my sleeve.

The church is silent. The song's over. I'm still standing.

I peek around the room. Everyone else in the congregation is already sitting down.

Immediately, I sink into the pew, lowering myself a few extra inches for good measure. A yard away, I feel the heat of my mother's eyes on me. Reaching for my program, I wave it in front of my red-hot face to block her stare.

Some things never change. I will always be Aubie's daughter, and she will undoubtedly, even when I am sixty and she is in her eighties, find something to correct about the way I look, act, or dress.

No way on earth will I share that I was thinking about Daniel.

Mama's had enough trouble getting used to that idea of me dating Billy.

It's not that Mama hasn't made her own share of poor choices, my father and hard liquor being among them.

My daddy, TJ, is in jail, doing much-deserved time for a variety of white collar crimes—in addition to plotting and executing the destruction of several Eufaula landmarks.

I've been to visit him once, but his detachment from reality is remarkable; his way of coping. On or off-season, he's focused on Auburn football, the team's current coach, and whether or not the Tigers will beat the Alabama Crimson Tide in next year's Iron Bowl.

If I had to guess, he keeps busy running numbers, and not just for SEC football. Other than construction, it's what he knows and loves.

Again, some things never change, though I have to admit that some good did come from the shock of my father's arrest.

It snapped my mother into giving up drinking. That, compiled with the realization Daddy'd been dating Mary Katherine—my brother's almost-fiancé—and we had several episodes worth of gossip for Wendy Williams' talk show.

After one trip to a high-end rehab center, remarkably, Mama has held her own. Sobering up means she's healthier, fifteen pounds lighter, and dating again. Although she's technically 'on the market,' she's head over heels for David Sullivan, a New York City magazine editor.

The two met in 1965, the first year of Eufaula's annual Pilgrimage, our city's annual tour of historic homes. The April event is a fundraiser to ensure preservation of the many antebellum mansions and landmarks from the era of cotton and confederate war.

According to both David, and my mother, Aubie, it was love at first sight, but my grandmother intervened, Romeo and Juliet style, to keep the two apart. The plan worked for forty-seven years, until MeeMaw realized the error of her ways and suspected my father of cheating—not only in business—but in his marriage.

When a developer threatened to raze a portion of the city's historic district and put up high-end condominiums, MeeMaw enlisted David's journalistic prowess to uncover the truth behind his plan. Along with his daughter Julia,

David helped save the town and won back my mother's heart in a span of twenty-four hours.

It's been nonstop romance from then on. In fact, David's flying in Christmas Eve from the City to spend the week with my mother in Eufaula. My brother's doing the opposite, heading north to enjoy the snow with David's daughter, Julia. We're all waiting for the big proposal, but so far, Shug hasn't popped the question.

There's little doubt in my mind that both my brother and my mother will be married and back from their honeymoons before Billy ever thinks about buying me an engagement ring.

He's entirely too content being non-committal.

And I've been too busy—or too chicken—to declare an ultimatum.

Besides, who wants to be alone on Christmas? Or spend New Year's Eve in front of the television watching the ball drop in Times Square?

Billy's parents are devout Christians and respected members of the community. His older brother's a Marine who came home from his last tour in Iraq with a chest full of medals, and his little sister is this year's reigning Miss Alabama.

All-American as you can get, right?

Not Billy.

We dated all through high school, then had a fight about the senior class prank, which involved letting a coop-full of chickens loose in the main building—after taking apart the principal's car and putting it back together on the roof of the school gym.

I voted absolutely not, he voted yes, and proceeded to get arrested. Twenty-four hours and one mug-shot later, he walked out of the local lock-up and I refused to speak with the guy who made the *Eufaula Tribune*'s front page.

Three months later, all charges were dropped, and instead of orange, Billy wore crimson and white, playing wide receiver for the University of Alabama. When the Tide football team began winning, all gossip about his prank disappeared, forgotten as quickly as morning fog burning off Lake Eufaula.

In Southern belle tradition, and on the firm advice of my mother, I fixed my makeup, kept my chin up, and began dating the next eligible bachelor in town. Several years later, Kenny Sweet—who ended up being anything but—was my next mistake.

After spending one long weekend in Destin, Florida, I was too sick to get out of bed. A few weeks later, I woke up and the room swam, I couldn't endure the scent of fresh-brewed coffee, and it was painfully obvious that my body was pinging with hormones in overdrive.

After a midnight trip to the closest open-all-night Walgreens pharmacy, my fate was confirmed.

My tearful confessional did nothing to instill confidence in Kenny. My baby daddy screamed out of town as fast as his four-wheel drive could go when I announced I was pregnant with his child. Last I heard, he was somewhere in Mississippi, shacked up with a sixty-year old former debutante who collects boy-toys on the side.

My mortified mother sent me away to "visit" family in Mississippi until Ella Rae made her debut. There was no big welcome, no baby showers, and I returned to Eufaula with no pomp or circumstance.

During the day, I took a secretarial job with Jordan Construction. Aubie watched Ella Rae, and we lived in the little carriage house behind my parent's home.

Baking became my release; a way to soothe my feelings and make me feel better about being a single mom. It started on trips to the Carnegie Library, while Ella Rae would read picture books, I'd wander over to the cookbooks and flip through the pages.

It was then I learned to really cook, practicing recipe after recipe in the safety and protection of my mother's kitchen. It began as a hobby, morphed into occasional requests from family for birthday cakes, then became a side business for weddings and special events like the Eufaula Pilgrimage.

Two years ago, before I knew Shug had planned on helping me start my own business, I was bringing in nearly equal amounts of income from Jordan Construction and the bakery. I'd become an entrepreneur without even realizing it.

After Ella Rae's Sweets opened, I wasn't looking to start dating again, but when word got out that the shop was a success, Billy—now an insurance agent—meandered back into town.

When he showed up at the bakery in late May, looking cleaned-up, well-dressed, and charming, I thought he'd changed. He begged me to talk, staring earnestly with his green eyes that make me melt like butter on a hot skillet.

And for a while, things were close to perfect. We dated—actually went out—to the movies, to dinner. He brought me flowers and remembered my favorite music. To my shock, he confessed that he loved me.

When the end of the summer rolled around, I braced myself for football season. To my surprise, Billy was only mildly addicted to his Saturday games, limiting his viewing time to exclusively SEC football. We'd see each other during the week. Standard dating practice in the Deep South from August through December.

That sport, though, I soon discovered, was the least of my problems.

I'd forgotten all about hunting season.

My girlfriends, the ones married to hardcore hunting

men like Billy, jokingly call it the widows' season. Most of them use shopping therapy to pass the time.

Me? Thank goodness I have the bakery.

This morning, Billy's out with his dogs trying to score his first big buck. More than once, he's asked me to come along, but I'm less than thrilled about the idea of sitting out in the woods, completely quiet, waiting for a four-legged beast with antlers to wander into the view of my boyfriend's scope.

I didn't even attempt to convince him to come to church —even to appease my mother. And knowing Billy, if we debated the issue, he'd argue that sitting up in his tree stand is his way of getting closer to God. Most men I know, including my father, wouldn't disagree.

My fingers tap on the wooden edge of the pew bench.

The sermon's drawing to a close.

I glance around, shaking away my dream-like state, and notice that Daniel's gone. Slipped away, sometime in the last twenty minutes.

Another twinge of worry seizes my chest.

I remind myself of his smile. He's got this. He promised. He has a plan.

Next to me, Ella Rae smothers a yawn and cuddles up against my shoulder. The warmth of my daughter's body courses through me, and I let myself relax in the moment. With a gentle hand, I reach up and stroke her soft curls.

Her fingers find my other hand and squeeze tight.

A surge of determination rushes through me. My mind begins to whirl with ideas.

On more than one occasion, Billy's promised to make it up to me—all of the time we've missed out on for SEC football and hunting season. In fact, last Wednesday, he told me he'd buy me whatever I wanted for Christmas. I just had to tell him.

I can save Ella Rae's Christmas from being a total disaster.

I can bring back the magic.

I just need a little help.

As we rise to sing the final hymn of the church service, I figure out exactly how my boyfriend of the moment can repay his little debt.

And then some.

CHAPTER 6

DECEMBER 23

"But, it will be fun," I plead, squeezing an even line of blue icing onto the edges of star-shaped sugar cutouts. It's a last minute order for a new customer, and he sounded quite desperate on the phone, asking that three dozen cookies be finished by tomorrow night for a "special occasion."

"PD, that's insane," Billy answers, obviously exasperated. "You know I don't like getting dressed up."

"It's for Ella Rae," I say, cradling the phone between my ear and shoulder as I pick up a different bag and add red piping to the baked-golden bells. "I want to prove that she doesn't have to listen to Arthur Cunningham."

He exhales into the phone and mutters something unintelligible. "That kid's a pain in the butt. He talks too much."

"I know," I say. "That's what I'm trying to undo. He listed off all this scientific and mathematical stuff about why it's impossible for Santa to deliver toys to kids around the world."

"He's too smart for his own good," Billy retorts.

"Honey, that's why I need your help," I say in my sweetest

voice. "It's Christmas Eve. Surely, you're not planning on going hunting tomorrow night."

It's a statement, not a question, but there's silence after the words come out of my mouth. I already know what he's going to say, and it involves four legs and hooves.

"Babe," he says. "I don't have my buck yet."

As I sprinkle silver nonpareils onto my Christmas tree-shaped cutouts, I swallow my frustration.

"I know it's important to you," I reply, surveying my work. I cap a jar of colored sprinkles. "And of course I know that you want your buck. Don't you have until the end of January?"

Billy doesn't realize I've memorized the Alabama Hunting and Fishing Digest calendar for Barbour County.

I hear a begrudging grunt. "Yeah, if I don't take the dogs."

"Okay, so," I say brightly. "All you have to do is show up and put on the suit."

More silence.

"The guys from the fire department offered to drive you in the new pumper truck. It'll only take thirty minutes, tops. The guys will just pull up in front, flashing the lights and sounding the sirens," I explain. "Ella Rae'll be so surprised, she'll be over the moon."

"Yeah, I guess she will be," Billy says, letting out a little laugh. He sounds more excited now that I've mentioned the fire truck and a half-hour time frame. "Fine, I'll do it."

I let out all of the air I've been holding in my chest. Thank. The. Lord.

"You're the best," I say.

"Just this once," Billy warns.

"I'll drop off everything you need tomorrow after lunch, okay?"

We hang up and I hug myself tight. Christmas might be saved, after all.

CHAPTER 7

*E*lla Rae's with my mother doing some last-minute shopping in Dothan, so the morning flies by. After the lunch rush, I make a phone call to the one person who can help me in any pinch:

Roger.

Our long-time family friend and local business owner is a genius when it comes to all things fashion. He's my go-to guy for balls and wedding attire, and every pageant princess worth knowing has Roger's number in her cell phone.

I hold my breath.

Three rings later and he picks up. I explain my Christmas dilemma, mincing details as best I can, and wrapping up the story with Billy's promise to help me.

"Oh, darling," he coos. "I love surprises. I have just the thing."

Ten minutes later, good as gold, he's standing in the doorway of his B & B, a long garment bag draped over the crook of his arm.

"Hey, gorgeous!" he calls, waving from the porch.

As usual, he's dressed immaculately, as if photographers

from GQ were descending on Eufaula within the hour for a cover shoot. His dark gray suit drapes beautifully, accented by a bright red tie and pocket square. Platinum cufflinks accent his wrists.

I park and bound up the stairs, breathless when I reach him.

Roger air kisses me on both cheeks. "Good to see you."

"Brought you a present," I say, holding up a small box of cutouts.

He clasps both hands to his chest and twists his lips to one side. "Oh, naughty girl. You shouldn't have. I have to watch my waistline."

I roll my eyes and hand him the box anyway. "Puh-lease," I say, exaggerating the word.

Smirking, he takes the gift, and then reaches forward with his fingertips. "You have a smidge of flour. Right here." Roger brushes my cheek and smiles. "There. All better."

"Hazard of the job," I grin.

"As is your outfit?" Roger raises an eyebrow, and then steps back to check out my attire. "Are you planning on baking for my guests, too?"

"Another time, my dear," I laugh, realizing that I didn't bother to take off the ruffled blue and yellow apron that's tied around my waist.

He chuckles. "I've got a full house. We'd love some crème Brule and pineapple upside down cake. Oh, maybe Bananas Foster." He claps his hands. "Yummy!"

"I love you to death, but the answer's no," I say firmly.

"Fine," Roger thrusts the garment bag into my waiting arms and pretends to be offended. "Are you sure Prince Might-Be-Charming-If-He-Shaved-Once-In-A-While is going to come through for you?"

"Don't even say that," I warn, feeling a surge of butterflies twirl in my stomach.

"Have a back-up *man*? I mean...plan?" He asks, batting his eyelashes. "I can help."

"Roger!" I say, poking him in the shoulder. "Billy promised."

My friend cocks his head and stops joking. "I know he did. And I know how important this all is to Ella Rae, that feisty little darling of yours. It'll break her heart if—" Roger summons a breath. "PD, I swear, If he screws this up, he'll have to answer to me."

I am a bit taken aback with the force of his statement. "Thank you," I say softly, and squeeze his hand.

With that, I'm back in the car. I head toward the outskirts of town, up Eufaula Street, past all of the homes dressed in their Christmas best. Wreathes with red velvet ribbon decorate every door. Garlands, thick and green, accent porch railings and stately columns. Single candles dot many windows. Behind them, Christmas trees sparkle in gold and silver splendor.

I drive across the bridge overlooking Lake Eufaula. The water shimmers in the sunlight, and a fish jumps as a pair of Sandhill cranes fly close to the surface, no doubt looking for a lunchtime snack.

After another mile, I turn left onto Gammage Road. Billy's house isn't far, and I'll leave the bag hanging on his porch if he's not home. I turn into his driveway and ease the car to a stop. His truck, parked askew in the front yard, is caked with mud from the tires to the undercarriage. His hunting gear and Yeti cooler are still in the back.

As I make my way up the gravel walk, I decide not to knock. He might be sleeping after traveling so much last week. He might be grumpy about the delivery, which I don't want to handle right now. The bottom line is that I have to get back to work. There's so much to do before tomorrow.

Without making a sound, I open the screen door, slip the hanger over the metal frame, and begin to step away.

Then, I hear it. A muffled giggle.

My eyes dart around the yard and back at my car. Am I hearing things? Was that a cat? The wind? A bird?

I hold myself perfectly still and don't breathe, listening again.

A moment later, there's another giggle. From inside Billy's house.

Closing my eyes, I count to ten. Then do it backwards.

This is not happening. I hug my arms across my chest, gripping my rib cage.

Is it his mother? A cousin I didn't know existed?

A sick ache rises in my chest because I know—for sure—that it's neither.

Suddenly, standing on my boyfriend's porch, exhausted, flour-covered, and in an apron, I realize that I am furious. Betrayed. Hurt. And mad as hell.

I don't bother to bang on the door. I don't yell or give him warning.

Quietly, calmly, I swallow my anger, turn the knob, and walk in.

"PD!" Billy yells. "What the hell?"

He's standing with his back to the front door, pants around his ankles.

From what I can tell, the girl who's with him is in an equal state of undress. Thankfully, most of her body remains covered by my boyfriend's backside.

Red-faced, and unable to budge from his awkward position, Billy spouts off a second question. "Don't you knock?"

"Didn't think I had to," I reply coolly.

"Good Lord Almighty," he mutters, looking away.

I almost choke at the reference. Really? A day before Christmas and that's all he can come up with?

"Unfortunately," I continue dryly. "*He's* not going to help you now. Either one of y'all."

And I turn on my heel, exit the house, and grab Roger's garment bag.

Just for fun, I leave the front door wide open.

CHAPTER 8

I don't cry until I get back to the shop. I make it all of the way inside, close the door behind me, flip the sign to 'closed,' and sink to the floor.

First, I call my mother.

She doesn't answer. Her voicemail clicks on almost immediately, a sure sign she and my daughter are still at the mall.

"Mama, can you please keep Ella Rae for a couple more hours?" I sniff, trying not to let a sob escape. "I had something—come up—an emergency. I'll come get her at eight, okay?"

I hang up and press the phone to my chest.

And let it all out.

An hour later, I've dried my tears. After examining my blotchy cheeks and red-rimmed eyes, I splash ice cold water on my face. The shock of the freezing liquid snaps me back into a semblance of reality.

I have customers waiting.

People are counting on me, including my daughter. I

don't have time for a pity party, much less a full-out break-down and hysterics.

Blotting my damp skin with a towel, I gaze back at my reflection in the mirror.

I can do this. I will.

I run a comb through my hair, gloss my lips, and open the front door.

In the back of the shop, I check my list and prepare the ingredients for Hummingbird cake and caramel apple pie. As I begin, my movements are jerky and awkward. I spill milk, drop a spoon on the floor, and knock over a salt shaker in the first five minutes.

Eventually though, I begin to breathe again. The routine of my work starts to soothe my fractured heart. Surrounded by the sights and smells of what I love, I lose myself in the rhythm of measuring and mixing.

The feel of soft white flour between my fingertips is comforting. When I add sugar, the crystals ping inside my bowl and sound like tiny church bells. A whiff of pure almond extract explodes my senses.

I'm so engrossed in my task that I don't realize Ted Hicks is standing at my counter, waiting patiently for me to notice him.

"Ted!" I jump, covering my mouth.

"Sorry, dear, I didn't want to interrupt." He laughs in a deep, booming baritone.

I brush my hands off on my apron and come around the counter to give him a quick hug. His shirt smells deliciously of cinnamon and nutmeg, Linda's favorite candle scents.

"Where's your lovely bride?" I ask, heading for the coffee pot.

"At home," he replies with a wry smile. "Looking after Arthur. His mom's working, bless her heart."

"The usual?" I ask, gesturing toward the dark roast.

He nods.

"What's on the agenda for today?" I ask, pouring the coffee in a to-go cup.

"A bit of miracle working," he says.

His words—and the absolute serious tone of his voice—make me stop. *Miracle working?* I turn to look at Ted and raise an eyebrow. "I could use some of that," I reply, handing his drink across the counter.

Ted sips thoughtfully. "'Tis the season."

I lean in on the counter and plunk down both elbows, resting my chin in my hands. "So, who's the lucky recipient? Are you taking applications?" I try to giggle, but the sound comes out too high-pitched and forced. Tears prick at the corners of my eyes and I have to stop talking to keep from crying.

"I keep thinking about Arthur and the Lego set. I want to —" Ted quits mid-sentence and frowns at me. "PD. What's wrong?"

Quickly, I shake my head, wipe at my lashes, and shrug it off. Without going into detail, I explain as simply as I can. "It's over with Billy. He decided to pursue some 'extra-curricular' activities." I make quotation marks in the air.

Not looking surprised in the least, Ted folds his arms across his broad chest. "I know that hurts. I'm sorry." He takes another sip of coffee. "You might not want to hear this, but the choice he made...it's for the best."

I manage a half-smile. "I know." And deep down, I do.

The truth is that Billy and I have little in common, we don't share the same goals, and dreams. He's not interested in settling down, being a step-father, or a husband, for that matter.

"What's the worst is that he screwed up my plans for surprising Ella Rae tomorrow night." I tell Ted about the Santa costume Roger lent me, the surprise fire truck visit, and Daniel's plan to try and secure the top gift on Ella's Christmas list. "Crazy, right?"

"Maybe it's not all going to work out like a storybook, PD," Ted says, after considering my explanation. "But you're doing the best you can. And despite all of your good intentions, Ella Rae will never know otherwise. She'll have a *good* Christmas. She has you as a mother."

"Thank you," I blush a little at the compliment.

Ted chuckles. "And as for things in the love department, I think you'll find what you're looking for when you least expect it," he says mysteriously. "In fact, there's probably someone already in your life, just waiting for you to notice him."

I scoff and wave Ted off. "Mm-hmm."

My friend raises his cup and looks up at the mistletoe hanging overhead. "I'll make a prediction."

Knitting my brow, I meet Ted's gaze.

"Here goes," he continues. "Tomorrow night, right in this very spot, someone will kiss you under the mistletoe."

For a moment, I can't breathe. Ted Hicks has lost his mind. What does he know that I don't? Who would waltz into my bakery and expect a kiss? On Christmas Eve?

He doesn't have a chance. "Oh, Ted Hicks, you have yourself a bet," I say.

He grins. "Good girl. The wager is this. If I win, you throw a New Year's Eve party at the bakery for our closest friends. If I lose, we'll ring in the New Year at my house. You won't have to lift a finger."

I can't help smiling. *Easy-peasy.*

"You've got yourself a deal."

CHAPTER 9

DECEMBER 24

*C*hristmas Eve day dawns bright and sunny, with a delicious chill in the air. I actually toss on a windbreaker and scarf before Ella and I walk out the door.

My daughter's insisted on wearing snow boots—just in case—and a fur trimmed hat and mittens. She's adorable, in a snow princess sort of way, though when we step outside, the trees, plants, and shrubs are just as green as the day before.

At the bakery, I plug in my iPod, scroll through to my Christmas soundtrack and hit shuffle. Music fills the air, immediately lifting my mood.

A steady line of happy customers streams in and out the door all day. I bag cookies, box up pie, and wrap gifts until my fingers ache. Ella Rae helps with the curling ribbon and fetching containers.

I'm so focused that Billy rarely crosses my mind, and when his face pops up in my brain, I firmly push it aside, choosing instead to sing along with Harry Connick Jr. to 'The Little Drummer Boy' and "Rudolph the Red-Nosed Reindeer.'

By mid-afternoon, the bakery shelves are almost bare,

47

and the shop's tip jar is overflowing with dollar bills and change. While I rearrange the remaining cakes, cookies, and tarts, I allow Emma to count out our earnings in the back room. She tackles the task with great interest, tucking a pen behind her ear and a small notebook under her arm.

I wipe down the countertops, re-brew coffee, and double-check that evening's few remaining deliveries are packaged and ready to go. Daniel's scheduled to come by shortly, and tonight, of all nights, I want to make sure that I don't slow him down.

As a thank you for all of his help over the past year, I've put together a basket with all of his favorites—red velvet cupcakes, a mini-pound cake, fresh biscuits, and a few jars of my homemade peach jam that I'd saved for him from this summer's harvest.

As I set the basket to one side, I notice that there's one order no one's claimed. The desperate, last-minute order for cutout sugar cookies. I check the receipt, but I can't recall the person's exact name, which sounded like 'Nole' or 'Nopole.'

I was in such a hurry, I didn't ask the man to spell it out—and neglected to jot down the phone number. Tucking the box next to Daniel's gift, I decide that if worse comes to worse, and no one shows up, it'll make a perfect present for Arthur and his mother. I'll simply drop it off on our way home tonight.

As the day creeps toward evening, and the shadows begin to lengthen, Ella Rae lets out a big yawn. She stretches her arms above her head and makes fists, closing her eyes.

All of a sudden, there's the chugging sound of an engine outside the shop and the loud honk of a truck horn.

"Daniel's here," I announce, although Ella Rae seems more interested in resting her head on the cafe table than checking out my UPS deliveries.

"Ho, ho, ho," a voice booms. Daniel, looking adorable in a

Santa hat and his UPS uniform, is standing in the doorway with a huge sack slung over his shoulder.

Ella Rae's head pops up.

I giggle.

"We're ready to go," he motions for us to follow him. "I have your hats." Daniel holds up matching red caps with white fur trim.

"Go where?" Ella Rae asks.

"We've been appointed," Daniel says, whipping out a sheet of paper. "Shortage of sleighs and elves this year. There's no time to waste!"

Ella Rae examines the official certificate, printed out on gold-trimmed paper. "For real?"

"It's an emergency," Daniel says, giving me a look that says *hurry*.

I take the cap, put it on my head, and settle it in place. "Let's go."

"Do you have the cookies?" Daniel asks, frowning. "The North Pole placed an order yesterday," he says, looking mischievous.

The name 'Nopole' or 'Nole' finally make sense. "Got it."

Daniel takes Ella Rae by the hand, I grab the cookies, and lock the door behind us. As I'm turning the key, I can hear my daughter exclaim in surprise.

The UPS truck is strung with holiday lights in every color, blinking and flashing. There are wreathes around both headlights, and the antlers and nose of a reindeer on the front grill.

We climb inside, and Daniel straps Ella Rae into the front passenger seat.

Over the next hour, we make stops all over Eufaula, handing out gifts and the Christmas cookies that Daniel ordered. Assisted by my daughter, Daniel rings doorbells and delivers packages to anxious parents, grandparents, and cousins.

Ella Rae's face is shining with happiness, aglow with seeing the joy at every doorstep, and happiness on all of the faces.

"There's one final stop we have to make," Daniel says, glancing back at me. The UPS truck turns onto Magnolia Street, and eases to a stop in between Ted and Linda Hicks' house and the Cunningham home.

"Which house?" Ella Rae asks.

Daniel doesn't answer at first, just smiles and goes to the back to retrieve a large, wrapped gift with a bow. He hands it to my daughter.

"Want to deliver it?" he says.

Ella Rae reads the card taped to the present and nods. As she unbuckles the belt and gets out of her seat, the box shakes and rattles.

Clutching it to her chest, she descends the truck's big steps, drops to the ground, and makes her way to Arthur Cunningham's porch. When she rings the bell, I can't breathe.

The wait goes on for two minutes, then three.

Finally, a porch light flickers, bathing the space in light. Arthur and his mother open the screen door.

lla Rae holds up the package and hands it to Arthur. I can't hear a word, but from the look on his face, it's evident there's been a change of heart about miracles and Santa Claus.

From the corner of my eye, I see movement next door. The Hicks are on their porch, watching the excitement.

"Did you?" I ask Daniel, who's paying very close attention to both households.

"Nope," he says, grinning.

"Did they?" I say, pointing at the Hicks.

Daniel puts a finger over his lips. "I can't tell you."

I settle back in my seat, content with his answer.

When Ella Rae returns, pink-cheeked, she claps her hands in excitement. "I think it was the Harry Potter set. Hogwarts Castle. Can you believe it?"

Daniel cranks the engine of the UPS truck and we rumble away. I take a last look at the Cunningham home, secure in the fact that my daughter is right.

Minutes later, we're back at Ella Rae's Sweets.

"Time to close up shop and go home," I announce to my daughter.

She glances at Daniel, who nods his agreement. We park and Ella Rae slowly steps out of the truck. Daniel doesn't seem to be in any hurry to leave. In fact, he jumps down and jogs around the other side of the truck to help my daughter make her way down the giant steps.

I hesitate. "Would you like to come in? I'll make you some hot cocoa to go with your cookies."

"They're all gone," he says, beaming anyway. "But I can make time for hot chocolate."

"Great," I say. My heart skips as I unlock the door and we step inside. Harry Connick Jr. is still singing, this time, one of my very favorites, 'O Holy Night.'

There's a wrapped gift in the center of the room, placed upright on one of the cafe tables. It's trimmed in silver and light blue, with curls of ribbon dripping from the center bow. Ella Rae's name is clearly marked on the square card, and my daughter approaches the box cautiously.

"For me?" she says, taking another step forward.

My heart thuds as I see the excitement on Ella Rae's face. In the rush and fun of delivering everyone else's presents, I'd almost forgotten Daniel's promise to find my daughter's number one gift.

He nods. "Santa knew we were busy with Arthur's present. He must have made a special trip from the North Pole—just for you."

Ella Rae picks up the box. She's careful, as if touching the wrapping paper might break the gift into pieces.

"Did you?" I whisper, looking up into Daniel's blue eyes.

We're standing so close that we're almost touching. An inch apart. I can feel his breath on my face. He's smiling.

"Maybe," he whispers back, putting an arm around my shoulders.

There's the sound of ripping paper, and Ella giggling, but it's all blurred by Daniel's touch. His hand on my bare skin radiates warmth, and I have to work extra hard to focus on the gift Ella Rae is unwrapping.

"It's the American Girl Doll I wanted," Ella Rae squeaks in delight. "Rebecca Rubin, with the accessories." She holds up the box with the doll inside. The Rebecca doll is gorgeous, with hazel eyes and honey-brown hair.

"She's beautiful," I say.

"Santa did know," Ella Rae murmurs to herself as she examines the gift. With a tiny squeal of excitement, she runs into my office and plops down on her pink bean bag chair. "This is the best Christmas, ever," she calls out.

"It is," Daniel agrees, drawing me closer.

I'm stunned. There's no American Girl store here. The closest shop is almost two hundred miles away. Daniel had to drive there and back in the last forty-eight hours, on no sleep, and the off chance the store might sell the last Rebecca doll on the shelf.

"How can I ever thank you—"

"I'd like the discount," he says with a grin.

Instantly, my body tingles. Daniel isn't joking. This is real.

It's then that I know Ted Hicks was right all along. My perfect someone was here the whole time. I just had to open my heart and realize it.

In the instant before his lips meet mine, I look up. We're under the mistletoe. As Daniel leans in, cupping my face in his hands, Harry Connick Jr. begins singing the last track on his album, "What are you doing New Year's?"

After a delicious, long, slow kiss, I am breathless. My head is spinning.

"Great song. Perfect timing," Daniel says, his breath warm on my ear. "Would you like to dance?"

I can't do anything but nod. He wraps his arms around

me, his hand on the small of my back. As we sway to the music, I snuggle in closer and lose myself in the moment.

Daniel sings along. *"What are you doing New Year's? New Year's Eve."*

As the notes fade and the song ends, Daniel gazes down at me. He doesn't release me from the embrace. I don't want him to let me go.

"Do you know how long I've been waiting to kiss you?" he asks, voice husky with emotion.

I flush pink and shake my head, unable to look away.

"Second grade. The day on the playground."

I let out a small gasp—half surprise and half delight at his admission—and bury my head in the warmth of his chest. His hand caresses my hair. Eventually, his fingers trail across my neck, finding my chin. He lifts my face to meet his.

"There's nothing I wouldn't do for you, PD," Daniel murmurs.

I smile, glowing with happiness.

"You saved Christmas," I say. "That, alone, is a miracle."

Daniel takes my hand in his. "One American Girl Doll isn't too much to ask."

At the mention of his gift, I realize we haven't heard a peep from my daughter. "We'd better check on Ella Rae," I say, flashing a quick smile. "Things are entirely too quiet for my liking."

Tiptoeing through the shop, Daniel and I ease our way to my office. As we peek around the corner, both of us muffle a laugh. My daughter is fast asleep on the bean bag chair, curled up with her Rebecca doll.

Her peaceful expression makes me think of Arthur Cunningham and his brand-new Lego set, Ted and Linda Hicks celebrating the season, Aubie enjoying Christmas with David, and my brother spending his holiday with Julia.

The clock on the wall chimes eleven times.

An hour until Christmas.

"We should get home," I whisper, not really wanting to leave.

Daniel's arm encircles my waist, drawing me closer once again. He kisses me softly, on the lips, my cheeks, and my nose.

"On one condition," he says playfully.

Immediately curious, I look up at Daniel and grin. "And that is...?"

"New Year's Eve," he says. "Be my date?"

I stand on my tiptoes, throw my arms around his neck, and hug him tight.

When I finally release him, he laughs. "I take it that's a yes?"

"Yes," I say with a wink. "And I know the perfect place to celebrate."

ACKNOWLEDGMENTS

To my wonderful family, Jami, Patrick, and John David, I love you! Hugs to Mom and Dad for offering endless encouragement.

My fantastic early readers include Maxine Kidder, Elizabeth Wright, and Jen McGee. Thank you.

I'm so grateful to the readers who've supported my Lauren Clark (and Laura McNeill) books and recommended them to others! You have my heartfelt gratitude. I love hearing from you—reach out to me anytime at laura@lauramcneill.com.

If you enjoyed *A Very Dixie Christmas*, please write a quick Amazon or GoodReads review. There's no greater compliment!

ABOUT THE AUTHOR

Lauren Clark writes sweet romance set in the Deep South. A former TV news anchor, Lauren adores flavored coffee, local bookstores, and anywhere she can stick her toes in the sand. Her big loves are her family, paying it forward, and true-blue friends.

Lauren is the author of several award-winning novels, including *Dancing Naked in Dixie, Pie Girls, Stardust Summer,* and *Stay Tuned.*

She also writes suspense novels under the name Laura McNeill. *Center of Gravity* and *Sister Dear* have been published by HarperCollins.

Visit Lauren's website at authorlaurenclark.com.

EXCERPT FROM DANCING NAKED IN DIXIE

CHAPTER 1

DANCING NAKED IN DIXIE

CHAPTER 1

"The new editor needs you, Julia." A stern summons from Dolores Stanley leaps over the cubicles and follows me like a panther stalking its prey.

"Just give me a minute," I beg with a wide smile as I sail by the front office and a row of hunch-shouldered executive assistants. Steaming Starbucks in hand, my new powder-white jacket stuffed in the crook of my arm, I give a quick wave over my shoulder.

I am, after all, late, a bit jet-lagged, and on deadline. A very tight deadline.

A glance at my watch confirms two hours and counting to finish the article. I walk faster. My heart twists a teensy bit.

I don't mean to get behind. Really, it just sort of happens.

However, that's all going to change, starting today. I'm going to organize my life, work, home, all of it. I'll be able to check email on the road, never miss an appointment, and keep up with all of my deadlines.

Just as soon as I can find the instruction manual to my new iPhone. And my earpiece.

Anyway, it's going to be great!

So great, that I'm not the least bit panicked when I round the corner and see my desk; which, by the way, is wallpapered in post-it notes, flanked by teetering stacks of mail, and littered with random packages. Even my voicemail light is flashing furiously.

Before I can take another step, the phone starts ringing.

In my rush to pick it up, I trip and nearly fall over a pile of books and magazines someone carelessly left behind. A thick travel guide lands on my foot and excruciating pain shoots through my toes. My coffee flies out of my hand and splats on the carpeting. I watch in horror as my latte seeps into the rug fibers.

"Darn it all!" I exclaim, snatching up the leaking cup and setting it on my desk. Other choice expressions shuttle through my brain as I catch the edge of the chair with one hand to steady myself. I frown at the offending mess on the floor. *Who in the world?*

Until it dawns on me. Oh, right. I left it all there in my hurry to make my flight to Rome. My fault. I close my eyes, sigh deeply, and the strap of my bag tumbles off my shoulder. Everything—keys, mascara, lip gloss, spare change—falls onto the desk with a huge clatter. Letters and paper flutter to the floor like confetti in the Macy's Day Parade. Just as Dolores sounds off again, her voice raspy and caffeine-deprived.

"*Now*, Julia."

My spine stiffens.

"Be right there," I call out in my most dutiful employee voice. Right after I find my notes and calm down.

As I start to search through my briefcase, a head full of thick silver curls appears over the nubby blue paneling.

"Hey, before you rush off," Marietta whispers, "how was Italy? Was it gorgeous, wonderful?"

"Marvelous," I smile broadly at my closest friend and conjure up a picture postcard of Rome, Florence, and sun-drenched Tuscany. Five cities, seven days. The pure bliss of nothing but forward motion. "From the sound of it, I should have stayed another day."

Marietta studies my face.

It's the understatement of the year. I hate to admit it, but the prospect of inhabiting an office cubicle for a week intimidates me more than missing the last connection from Gatwick and sleeping on the airport floor. Claustrophobia takes over. I actually get hives from sitting still too long. Most days, I live out of suitcases. And couldn't be happier!

I'm a travel writer at *Getaways* magazine. Paid for the glorious task of gathering fascinating snippets of culture and piecing them into quirky little stories. Jet-setting to the Riviera, exploring the Great Barrier Reef, basking on Bermuda beaches. It's as glamorous and exhilarating as I imagined.

Okay, it is a tad lonely, from time to time, and quite exhausting.

Which is precisely why I have to get organized. Today.

I sink into my chair and try to concentrate. What to tackle first? Think, think.

"Julia Sullivan!"

Third reminder from Dolores. Uh-oh.

Marietta rolls her eyes. "Guess you better walk the plank," she teases. "New guy's waiting. Haven't met him yet, but I've heard he's the 'take no prisoners' sort. Hope you come back alive."

All of a sudden, my head feels light and hollow.

I've been dying to find out about the magazine's new editor.

Every last gory detail.

Until now.

"I'm still in another time zone," I offer up to Marietta with a weak smile. My insides churn as I ease out of my chair.

Marietta tosses me a wry look. "Nice try. Get going already, sport."

I tilt my head toward the hallway and pretend to pout. When I glance back, Marietta's already disappeared. Smart girl.

"Fine, fine." I tug a piece of rebellious auburn hair into place, smooth my suit, and begin to march. My neck prickles.

I'm not going to worry. Not much anyway.

My pulse thuds.

Not going to worry about change. Or a re-organization. Or pink slips.

Focus, Julia.

The last three editors adored me.

At least half of the North American Travel Journalist Association awards hanging in the lobby are mine.

The best projects land in my lap. Almost always.

Well, there was the one time I was passed over for St. Barts, but I'm sure what's-her-name just had PMS that day. And I did get Morocco in February.

This last trip to Italy? Hands-down, one of the choice assignments.

I round the corner and come within an inch of Dolores Stanley's bulbous nose. As I step back, her thin red lips fold into a minus sign. Chanel No. 5 wraps around me like a toxic veil.

Dolores is the magazine's oldest and crankiest employee. Everyone's afraid of her. To be perfectly honest, Dolores doesn't like *anyone*, except Marietta—and the guy in accounting who signs her paycheck. And that's only twice a month.

Most of the office avoids her as if she's been quarantined

with a deadly virus. "Good morning, Dolores," I say with forced cheer.

As expected, she ignores me completely. Instead, Dolores heaves her purple polyester-clad bottom up off the chair, and lumbers toward the editor's office. Breathing hard, she pushes open the huge mahogany door, frowns, and tosses in my name like a careless football punt.

I follow the momentum, shoulders back, hoping Dolores doesn't notice my shaking hands.

Stop it, Julia. No worries, right?

Dolores pauses and murmurs something that sounds like 'good luck.' *Wait. Dolores wished me luck?* That freaks me out completely. I want to run. Or fall to the floor, hand pressed to my forehead, prompting someone to call the paramedics.

Too late. The door clicks shut behind me. The office already smells different. Masculine, earthy, like leather and sand. I crane my neck to see the new person's face, but the high-back chair blocks my view; an occasional tap-tap on a keyboard the only sound in the room.

I fill my lungs, exhale, and wait.

Light streams onto the desk, now piled high with newspapers, memos, and several back issues of *Getaways*. A navy Brooks Brothers jacket hangs in the corner.

I gaze out the window at the majestic skyscrapers lining Broadway, a blur of activity hidden behind a silver skin of glass and metal. A short ride away, three international airports bustle with life. Jets ready to whisk me away at a moment's notice. My pulse starts to race just thinking about it.

"Not in a big hurry to meet the boss?"

The gruff voice startles me. My knees lock up.

"Sir?" I play innocent and hope he'll blame Dolores.

The chair spins around. Two large feet plop on the desk and cross at the ankles. My eyes travel up well-dressed legs, a starched shirt, and a red silk tie. They settle on a pair of dark eyes that almost match mine.

For a moment, nothing works. My brain, my mouth, I can't breathe. It absolutely, positively may be the worst shock-of-my-life come true.

"David?" I stutter like a fool and gather my composure from where it has fallen around my feet.

The broad, easy grin is the same. But the hair is now a little more salt than pepper. The face, more weather-beaten than I remember.

"I told them you'd be surprised." David's face flashes from smug to slightly apologetic.

I say nothing.

"They talked me out of retirement," David folds his arms across his chest and leans back. "Said they *had* to have me."

"I'll bet," I offer with a cool nod.

His face reveals nothing. "Not going to be a problem, is it?"

Of course, it is! I dig my fingernails into my palm, shake my head, and manage to force up the corners of my mouth.

"Good." David slides his feet off of the desk and thumbs through a pile of magazines.

I stand motionless, watching his hands work. The familiar flash of gold is gone. I glower at his bare finger, incensed to the point of nearly missing all that he is saying. I watch David's mouth move; he's gesturing.

"…and so, we're going to be going in a new direction." He narrows his gaze. "Julia?"

I wrench my eyes up. "A new direction," I repeat in a stupid, sing-song voice.

David frowns. With a smooth flick of his wrist, he tosses a copy of *Getaways* across the desk. He motions for me to take it.

"The latest issue," he says.

Gingerly, I reach for it. And choke. *That's funny.* I purse my lips. *Funny strange.* The cover story was supposed to be mine. My feet start to tingle. I want to run.

Instead, I force myself to begin paging through for the article and stunning photos I'd submitted—shots of the sapphire-blue water, honey-gold beaches, and the lush green landscape.

With forced nonchalance, I search through the pages. *Flip. Flip. Flip.* In a minute, I'm halfway through the magazine. No article. No Belize. No nothing. My fingers don't want to work anymore. I feel sick.

"Julia, what is it? You seem a little pale," David prods. He leans back in his chair and stares at me with an unreadable expression.

I continue looking. *Where* is my article? Buried in the middle? Hidden in the back? More pages. I peek up at David, who meets my dismay with a steady gaze.

What kind of game is he playing?

I yank my chin up. "No, nothing's wrong," I say lightly, "not a thing."

Inside, I'm screaming like a lunatic. *There must be a mistake.* My bottom lip trembles the slightest bit. I blink. Surely, I'm not going to...lose my...

"It was junk. Pure and simple," David interrupts, the furrows on his forehead now more pronounced. He jumps up and folds his arms across his chest. "Bland, vanilla. The article screamed boring. It was crap."

Crap? Don't mince any words, David. He might as well toss a bucket of ice water on my head. I shiver, watching him.

"Let me ask you this." David stops walking back and forth and puts his fists on the desk. "How much time did you actually spend writing and researching the article? Just give me a rough estimate. In hours or days?" David's finished making his point. He sits down and begins glancing through a red folder.

My mind races. Last month? Right. Trip to Belize.

Focus. Try to focus.

I fidget and tap out an uneven rhythm with my shoe. Excuses jumble in my head, swirling like my brain is on spin cycle.

David clears his throat. He opens a manila envelope, thumbs through the contents, then gazes at me with the force of a steam-driven locomotive. "Are you taking care of yourself? Taking your … prescriptions?"

The words cut like a winter wind off the Baltic Sea.

I grope for words. My thoughts fall through my fingers.

My attention deficit isn't exactly a secret. Most everyone knows it's been a problem in the past. But, things are under control … it's all been fine.

Until now.

I start to seethe. David continues to gaze intently and wait for my reply.

What are you, a psychiatrist? I want to spout. *Not to mention all of the HR rules you're breaking by asking me that.*

"I'm off the medication. Doctor's orders. Have been for several years," I answer, managing to give him a haughty *the-rest-is-none-of-your-business* stare.

David backs off with a swivel of his chair. "Sorry. Just concerned," he says, holding one cuff-linked hand in the air. "So, *exactly* how much *time* did you *spend* on the *article?*" David enunciates each word, stabbing them through my skin like daggers.

"Five hours," I blurt out, immediately wishing I could swallow the words and say twelve. "Maybe seven."

David makes a noise. Then, I realize he's laughing. At me. At my enormous fib.

My face is scarlet, glowing hot.

Head bent, David flips through a set of papers. He pauses at a small stack. I recognize the coffee stain on one edge and the crinkled corner. My article.

"Let me quote verbatim to you, Ms. Sullivan," he says, his tone mocking. "Belize offers the best of both worlds, lovely beaches and a bustling city full of good restaurants. Visitors can find fascinating artwork and treasure hunt for souvenirs downtown."

He stops.

Surely, my article was better. He must have the draft. Oh, there wasn't a draft. Oops. Because I hadn't allowed myself much time. Come to think of it, I banged most of it out on the taxi ride from the airport. I accidentally threw away most of my notes in a shopping bag, which wasn't really my fault. I was late for my plane. And then…

"So, I killed it." David ceremoniously holds the papers over the trash can and lets go.

I watch the white papers float, then settle to their final resting place. Maybe I should jump in after them? My legs start to ache. Why did I wear these stupid Prada boots that pinch my left heel?

"But, all is not lost," David says dramatically. "I'll give you a chance to redeem yourself." He drums his fingers on the desk. "If you can up the caliber of your writing. Spend some time. Put your heart into it."

I don't say a word. Or make a sound. Because if I do, I'm sure to sputter out something I'll regret. Or, God forbid, cry. *Redeem myself? Put my heart into it?*

Deep breath. Okay, I can afford to work a teensy bit harder. Give a tad more effort here and there. But, the criticism. Ouch! And coming from David, it's one hundred times worse. The award-winning super-journalist who circled the globe, blah, blah, blah.

David cracks his knuckles. "Look, I know it's been tough

since your mother's illness and all." His tone softens slightly. "Her passing away has been difficult for everyone."

I manage not to leap over the desk and shake him by the shoulders. *Difficult? How would he know?* My blood pressure doubles. *Stay calm. Just a few more minutes.* Doesn't he have some other important meeting? An executive lunch?

David drones on like he's giving a sermon. I try to tune him out, but can't help hearing the next part.

"Julia, it's affected your writing. Immensely. And look at you. You've lost weight. You're exhausted. I want you to know I understand your pain—"

"You *don't* understand," I cut in before I can stop myself. My mother died two years ago. She was sick before that. I still miss her every day. *Damn him. Get out of my personal life. And stay out.*

We stare each other down, stubborn, gritty gunfighters in the Wild West.

"Fine," David says evenly and breaks my gaze. "So, as you've heard, the magazine is going in a new direction. The focus group research says …" He glances down at some scribbled notes. "It says our American readers want to see more 'out of the way' places to visit. Road trips. A Route 66 feel, if you will."

Focus groups. I forgot all about that obsession.

David pauses to make sure I'm listening. For once, he has my undivided attention.

"According to the numbers, they're saturated with Paris, London, the Swiss Alps. They want off the beaten path. Local flavor. So, we're going to give it a shot. We'll call it something like 'Back Roads to Big Dreams.'"

What a horrible idea. I swallow hard. Our readers don't want that! Who did he interview in these focus groups? The Beverly Hillbillies?

David continues, immensely pleased with the concept.

"The emphasis is going to be on places that offer something special—perhaps historically or culturally. But the town or city must also be looking toward the future. Planning how to thrive, socially and economically. It's going to be part of a new series, if it turns out well." David puts emphasis on 'if' and shoots me a look. "What do you think?"

Is he joking? He doesn't want my opinion. Does he honestly think I like the idea?

David pauses. Apparently, he expects a response. An intelligent, supportive one.

"Sounds ... interesting," I manage to squeak out and shift uncomfortably. I predict that I'll be spending a full day spinning half-truths. I'll likely be offered a lifetime membership in Deceivers Anonymous if I don't die first.

David snatches up his glasses. *Glasses?* When did he start wearing glasses?

"I know you're our token globe-trotter, but I'd hoped you'd be more enthusiastic." He taps his Mont Blanc on his desk calendar and then points to the enormous wall atlas. "I'm thinking Alabama."

Something massive and thick catches in my throat. My head swivels to the lower portion of the map. I begin to cough uncontrollably.

Ever so calmly, David waits for me to quit.

When I catch my breath, my mind races with excuses. The words stumble out of my mouth, tripping over themselves. "But, I have plans. Tickets to the Met, a fundraiser, a gallery opening, and book club on Monday." I don't mention the Filene's trip I'd planned. Or the romantic date I've been promising Andrew, my neglected boyfriend.

David waves a hand to dismiss it all. "Marietta can handle the magazine-related responsibilities."

From the top drawer of his desk, he produces an airline ticket and a folder with my name on it. He sets them on the edge of his desk. Something I can't decipher plays on his lips.

I keep my voice even. "What about Bali?" I had planned to leave for the South Pacific a week from Friday. "It's on my calendar. It's been on there…"

David shakes his head. "Not anymore."

The words wound me like a thousand bee stings.

"Alabama," David repeats.

I swallow, indignant. He's plucked me off a plum assignment without a thought to my schedule. My new boss is sending me to who-knows-where, and he looks perfectly content. I narrow my eyes and fold my arms.

"Seriously David, you're sending me on an assignment to…Alabama? *Alabama?*" I sputter, searching my brain for an appropriate retort. "I'd rather—I don't know—*dance naked* for my next assignment than go to Alabama!"

The announcement comes out much louder than I intend and reverberates through the room. Dolores probably has her ear pressed to the door, but the phrase bounces off my boss like a cotton ball.

David smothers a chuckle. "Suit yourself."

"It's a done deal, isn't it?" I finally manage, my voice low and uneven. The answer is obvious. The airline ticket and folder are within my grasp. I don't move a centimeter toward them. For all I know, the inside of one of them is coated with Anthrax. For a brief moment, I picture myself, drawing one last ragged breath, on the floor of David's brand-spanking-new office carpeting.

"It's your choice." David swipes at his glasses and settles them on his nose. "Deadline's a week from today. That's next Wednesday. Five o'clock. Take it or leave it."

I stifle an outward cringe at his tone, and the way he's spelling it out for me. Syllable by syllable, like I'm a toddler caught with my hand in the cookie jar.

Take it or leave it.

Not the assignment. My job.

It's your choice.

David's fingers hit the keyboard. Click-clack. "Oh, and leave your notes on Italy with Dolores. I'll write the article myself."

That's it. The meeting's over. I'm fuming. Furious. I want to rip up the papers an inch from his face and let a hailstorm of white scraps fall to the carpet.

Take it or leave it.

I start to turn on my heel and walk out like we'd never had the conversation. David will come around, won't he?

Then, I stop. It's a joke. An awful, terrible joke. Do I have other job prospects? Do I want to change careers? What about my apartment? What about the bills?

Fine. Okay. Have it your way, David.

I catch myself before I stick my tongue out. He probably has surveillance cameras set up on a 24-hour loop.

David knows I'm beaten.

So, I bend, ever so slightly. In one quick motion, I reach out to tuck the folder and ticket under my arm. In slow motion, the papers slip through my fingers like water between rocks in a stream.

Damn! The clatter of David's awkward typing stops.

So much for a smooth exit.

On the ground lies a square white envelope and matching note card. I swoop down to gather my mess.

Though I'm trying not to notice, I can't help but stare at the delicate pen and ink lines on the front of the card. There's no lettering, just thin strokes of black that form the outline of a majestic mansion and its towering columns. Before I can stop myself, I flip open the note card, expecting a flowery verse or invitation. Some event I'll be expected to attend for the magazine? A party?

There are only a few sentences inside, barely legible, scrawled in loopy, old-fashioned writing. *David, Please help*, I can make out. Underneath, a scribbled signature. An *M*, maybe?

Hmph. There's no end to what people will do to get a story. Gifts, money, flowers, I've seen it all. Traded for a snippet of publicity.

I refold the note and hand it across the desk. It must not be particularly important, because David takes the card and sets it aside without glancing at it.

Necessary papers tucked securely in the crook of my arm, I straighten up, flick an imaginary piece of lint off my skirt with my free hand, and begin to walk out. My feet brush the carpet in small, level steps.

I reach for the doorknob, inches from the hallway.

"Have fun! Don't forget to check in," David calls after me. "Oh, and send a postcard."

I scowl. His voice is ringing in my ears.

That's low. Lower than low. He knows I collect postcards. Make that *used to*. In my past life. I want to stomp out—have a proper four-year-old temper tantrum. Be in control, I tell myself. Keep your chin up. Walk.

David can go to Hell!

I make the most horrible, gruesome face I can think of. Surveillance cameras be damned.

Visit Amazon or BN.com to
purchase your copy of *Dancing Naked in Dixie*.